Whatever Is Lovely

Susie Poole

Text and illustrations © 2014 Susie Poole.
Published in 2017 by B&H Publishing Group,
Nashville, Tennessee
ISBN: 978-1-4627-4523-4
Dewey Decimal Classification: CE
Subject Heading: PRAYER \ WORRY
All rights reserved. Printed in Shenzhen, Guangdong, China.
1 2 3 4 5 6 7 8 • 21 20 19 18 17

B&H KIDS
Nashville, Tennessee

There are **things** that make me feel ...

afraid!

And **things** that make me
sad.

And sometimes
life seems so

unfair!

But I won't worry about these things. I'll talk to God and He'll help me.

And then . . .

I'll think about **whatever is lovely.**

I'll think about things that are . . .

amazing.

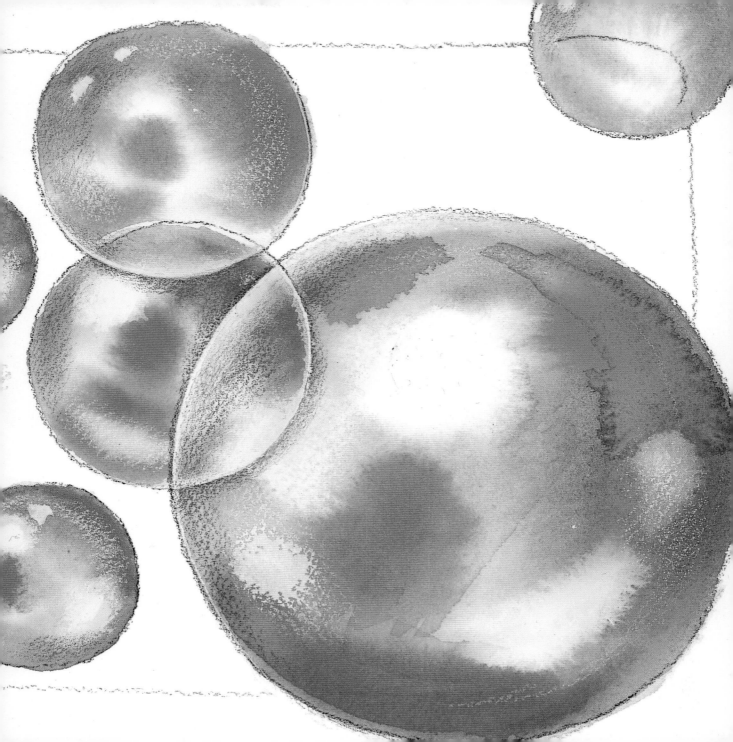

Things very **great.**

Things very . . .

small.

I'll think about
someone who is kind.

And how I can be kind, too.

Because this
makes God
happy.